MR. SNOW

by Roger Hargreaves

PS.S!
PRICE STERN SLOAN

One night, two days before Christmas, it started to snow.

All night it snowed and snowed and snowed and snowed and snowed.

Millions and billions and trillions of big, white, soft snowflakes covered the whole, wide world.

When morning came, it was quite amazing to see just how much snow had fallen.

All the houses, all the trees, all the roads, and all the fields were covered.

It was almost as if a huge, white blanket had been gently laid over everything.

Everywhere you looked was white!

And then the sun came out!

And so did the children!

They were all dressed up and muffled up, wearing scarves and coats and gloves and boots so that they wouldn't catch cold.

All the children were so excited to see so much snow, which isn't surprising really because there was more snow than they'd ever seen before.

Some of them went on their sleds, racing down the hills.

Some of them, who didn't have sleds, threw snowballs at each other.

One little boy even made a snowball that was as big as himself.

And some of the children made snowmen!

Then it was Christmas Eve.

The children all went home early so that they could go to bed early so that they could get up early to see what Santa Claus had brought them.

But that particular Christmas Eve, Santa Claus was in trouble.

And the trouble was that it had snowed so much that Santa Claus was stuck.

Really and truly stuck!

There was so much snow that his reindeer simply couldn't pull his sleigh piled high with all the presents that he had to deliver to all the children.

He sat down on his sack of toys and thought and thought how he could manage to deliver all the presents to all the children before they woke up on Christmas morning.

"Oh dear!" he said out loud, and sighed. "Oh dear me. What am I to do?"

Now, it just so happened that Santa Claus had gotten himself stuck just beside a snowman which one of the children had built.

And that gave him an idea.

A good idea.

A very good idea.

A very good idea indeed.

"How would you like to help me?" he asked the snowman.

But of course the snowman didn't answer because snowmen can't talk, can they?

"Of course, I'll have to use some of my magic to bring him to life," thought Santa Claus to himself.

So, he tugged his white beard three times and muttered some Santa Claussy magic words into it.

Suddenly, you might almost say magically, the snowman did come to life.

"Hello, Santa Claus," said Mr. Snow, which was the snowman's name. "You look a bit stuck if you ask me, which you didn't, but I'll say so anyway, and if you ask me again, I'd say you need a helping hand, if you know what I mean, which you probably do, because that's probably why you've brought me to life, which you certainly did, so can I be of any assistance?"

Mr. Snow, as you might have gathered, was a rather talkative sort of snowman.

"Exactly!" beamed Santa Claus. "Let's get started!"

And start they did.

Mr. Snow gave Santa Claus an enormous push and off they went.

They divided the work between them.

It was Mr. Snow's job to make sure that all the right toys for all the right boys, and all the right toys for all the right girls, were put into all the right sacks.

It was Santa Claus' job to make sure he took all the right sacks down all the right chimneys and delivered all the right toys to all the right boys and all the right toys to all the right girls.

Mr. Snow and Santa Claus made sure that Susan got her teddy bear.

Mr. Snow and Santa Claus made sure that John got his piggy bank.

Mr. Snow and Santa Claus even made sure that little Jane got her squeaky, pink elephant to play with in the bath.

And then, all of a sudden, they discovered that, between them, they'd finished.

"I'd like to thank you very much indeed for helping me deliver all the right toys to all the right boys," said Santa Claus, shaking Mr. Snow by the hand.

"Not forgetting all the right toys to all the right girls," replied Mr. Snow, shaking Santa Claus by the hand.

"And now I'd better turn you back into a snowman again," said Santa Claus. "Thank you again, and good-bye!"

"My pleasure!" smiled Mr. Snow.

And do you know, from that Christmas to this Christmas, Santa Claus always chooses a snowman to help him.

So the next time you build a snowman, you'd better make sure you build him properly, because somebody you know might want that snowman to give him a hand.